The Creator's Game

A STORY OF

Baaga'adowe / Lacrosse

Art Coulson

Illustrations by
Robert DesJarlait

Minnesota Historical
Society Press

For Sally Mills Rackliff, Cherokee mother, grandmother, healer, and storyteller —AC

Maa-Wiijiiwaagan miinawaa Niijaanisag —RD

CLEAN
WATER
LAND &
LEGACY
AMENDMENT

www.mhspress.org

The Minnesota Historical Society Press is a member of the Association of American University Presses.

Manufactured in the United States of America

10 9 8 7 6 5 4 3 2 1

♾ The paper used in this publication meets the minimum requirements of the American National Standard for Information Sciences—Permanence for Printed Library Materials, ANSI Z39.48–1984.

International Standard Book Number
ISBN: 978-0-87351-909-0 (paper)

Library of Congress Cataloging-in-Publication Data

Coulson, Art, 1961–
   The creator's game : a story of baaga'adowe/lacrosse / Art Coulson ; [illustrated by] Robert DesJarlait.
      pages cm
   Summary: "The game of lacrosse is a gift from the Creator, given to the American Indians in the long ago. But Travis Skinaway doesn't know the full story of the game: he only knows that he struggles to catch the ball and tends to throw it over the other boys' heads. Maybe he's not built right to run the field. His teammates and coach seem to think he's hopeless, anyway. Travis is ready to hang up his gear, but then his grandfather appears in a dream, explaining to him that lacrosse is a spiritual quest, just like a prayer, a song, or a dance. Mom doesn't believe Travis's story, but Grandma knows: she says dreamtime is just as real as awake time. Grandpa continues to visit Travis, sharing details about the different styles of play, the types of equipment, the various traditions among the tribes. Wearing his grandfather's gear, Travis gains confidence as he practices with the team. When opportunity strikes at the big game, he carries the durable weight of tradition onto the field with him, celebrating skills handed down through generations. Co-owner of Redbird Media and Design, Art Coulson (Cherokee) is an award-winning writer and editor with decades of experience playing lacrosse. Robert DesJarlait (Anishinaabe, Red Lake), cofounder of Protect Our Manoomin, is an artist and activist who illustrated Meridel LeSueur's *Sparrow Hawk*."— Provided by publisher.
   Summary: "Eleven-year-old Travis Skinaway learns about his American Indian culture and history as he practices the Creator's game, lacrosse."— Provided by publisher.
   Includes bibliographical references.
   ISBN 978-0-87351-909-0 (pbk.)
   1. Ojibwa Indians—Games—Juvenile literature. 2. Ojibwa mythology—Juvenile literature. 3. Lacrosse—Juvenile literature. I. DesJarlait, Robert, illustrator. II. Title.
   E99.C6C844 2013
   977.004'97333—dc23
                                    2013027765

The Creator's Game

"Hey! Don't throw it to him— he'll never catch it. He's terrible."

Travis looked down at the grass and tried to hide his red cheeks and ears as his teammates ran down the field toward the goal. He hated lacrosse practice. In fact, he hated lacrosse. He didn't know why Mom and Grandma insisted that he play the stupid game anyway.

"Skinaway, you're a midfielder! Run up the field when we have the ball. Give your teammates someone to throw to. C'mon, hustle!" Coach Deeley, a tall man with a red face and unruly hair the color of dry straw, was always yelling at Travis.

Travis, a sixth grader and beginning lacrosse player, shook his head to clear the sweat from his eyes and jogged down the uneven field. As Travis approached the goal, Tommy Fiorella threw the hard rubber ball at him. Before Travis could get his stick up to catch it, the ball bounced off his face mask and hit the turf.

Coach Deeley kicked the turf and blew his whistle. "That's it, boys. Practice is over."

"See, Tommy, I told you the klutz couldn't catch it," yelled Barry Amos as he ran for the sideline. Travis hated it when the boys made fun of his awkwardness. He shoved his gloves, pads, and helmet into his small gym bag and trudged to his grandma's car, idling loudly in the school parking lot.

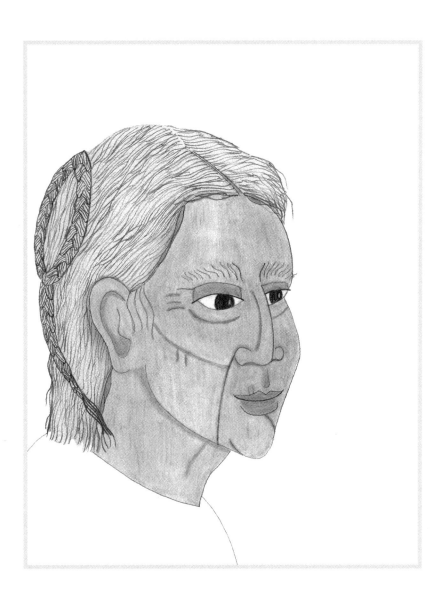

"How was practice?" Mom asked, as Travis pushed the beans and macaroni around on his plate. His grandma shot her a look and changed the subject.

"Any homework tonight? You need to keep up in school," Grandma said.

"No, I did all my homework before practice. I just want to go to bed and read my comic books," Travis replied. "I don't even want to think about stupid lacrosse. I don't know why I have to play a game I don't even like."

"Hey!" Grandma said. "Don't talk that way. Your grandpa, *Nenookaasii,* was a great lacrosse player. He was so fast and hard to catch, everyone at Leech Lake called him the Hummingbird. He was a strong, swift player. You will be, too. It's in your blood."

"No, I won't," Travis snapped. "I'm too slow and klutzy to play that game."

He walked the three steps to his bedroom and slammed the door. The thin paneled walls shook.

"Travis Skinaway!"

"Leave him," Grandma said, standing up to help her daughter finish clearing the small table. "He'll be okay."

Travis flopped down on his bed. He leaned over the edge and grabbed a tattered copy of *The Sandman: Dream Country* from his floor. He read for a long time, lying propped up on his pillows. He no longer heard the clatter of dishes and his mom and grandma talking in hushed voices.

When he got tired, Travis laid the comic on his nightstand and sat up to kick off his shoes. As the sneakers clunked to the floor, his grandpa stepped out of the shadows near his closet. He sat down on the edge of Travis's bed and touched the boy's face. Grandpa always smelled like strong coffee and Old Spice aftershave.

"What's this I hear about you wanting to quit lacrosse? Don't you know that game is in our blood as Anishinaabe people?"

Travis nodded his head. "I know, Grandpa, but I stink at it."

"You know why we play the game, don't you? *Baaga'adowe* is more than a game. It's the Creator's Game—we play for his amusement," Grandpa explained. "Indian people see lacrosse as a spiritual ceremony, like a prayer, a song, or a dance. We play it when people are sick, like medicine. We play it when we have something to celebrate. And also we play it to have fun. Now pull those covers up, shut off your light, and get some sleep. I'll see you soon, *Waabooz*."

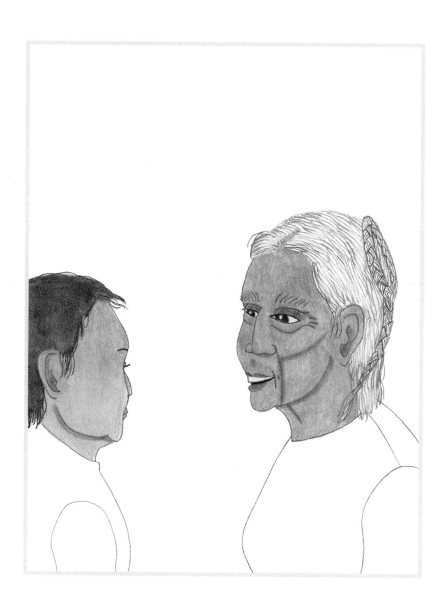

The smell of toast and frying bacon woke Travis. He dressed quickly, ran his fingers through his black hair, and walked out to the table. Grandma perched like a bird over her warm mug of coffee, with her feet on the seat of her chair and her knees bent up under her nightgown.

"How did you sleep?" Mom asked as she brought a plate to him.

"Great," Travis said between bites. "Grandpa told me a lot about lacrosse and why it's so important to us."

His mother stopped and turned to look at him. "You were dreaming, Trav. Your grandfather died a long time ago."

"No, Mom, I talked to him last night. He was here. He looked just the same as he always did."

"It was a dream. They can seem very real. I still dream about him sometimes, too."

Mom began slicing some cheese from the block on the counter.

Grandma leaned over to Travis and wrapped a thin arm around the boy's shoulder.

"You did see your grandfather," she whispered. "I believe you. Sometimes grownups forget. Dreamtime is just as real as awake time. Adults just don't want to believe it."

Travis nodded, then took a sip of his milk.

"You can learn a lot from your dreams, if you will only pay attention and listen," Grandma said. She smiled at him and winked. "Now hurry up and get your bag. I'll meet you out in the car. You don't want to be late again."

The afternoon sun warmed the grass as the boys who made up the Eagle Ridge sixth- and seventh-grade lacrosse team strapped on pads, put on their practice jerseys, and pulled helmets onto their heads.

"Line it up for passing drills," Coach Deeley called.

Billy Devine, the boy across from Travis, flicked his stick and tossed Travis the ball. To Travis's surprise, he caught it. Proud of himself for a change, Travis cradled the stick with his thick gloves and threw the ball back to Billy. But he released the ball too soon and watched, embarrassed, as it soared over Billy's head and bounced into the teachers' parking lot.

"Idiot," Tommy said, laughing as Billy turned to run after the ball. Travis wanted to burrow deep into the turf, like an earthworm.

Coach Deeley made a note on his clipboard and shook his head.

Forty-five minutes later, after drills and a short scrimmage, Travis was more discouraged than he had been the day before. He took off his gear and threw it into his bag.

He could see Grandma in her dull blue car with its rust around the grill. He walked slowly toward the car, his shoulders drooping and his stick dragging along the ground behind him.

"Another bad day, huh? Get in. We're having tacos for dinner and I'm hungry."

Travis slumped in his seat and stared out the window as the city rolled by.

After dinner, Travis and his grandmother sat together in her big worn recliner while Mom put away the taco fixings in the kitchen. The TV, playing a game show, cast its flickering light on the dark walls.

"Grandma, can I ask you something?"

"Sure, *Waabooz*. If I don't know the answer, I'll make something up."

"Tell me about Grandpa. I remember him . . . kind of. What was he like?" Travis turned toward Grandma, his eyes sparkling.

"Hand me that photo album under the table there," said Grandma, pointing to a thick brown vinyl book. She opened the album to a page of faded black-and-white photos. "This is a picture of your grandpa. Look at that beautiful dark hair. And those eyes. Ahhh. Every girl in Ball Club wanted to be his girlfriend. But I was the only one quick enough to catch the Hummingbird."

"The only one sweet enough," laughed Mom in the kitchen.

"Your grandfather was the best ball player at Leech Lake, probably in all the state. People came from every reservation in Minnesota and Wisconsin—some even came all the way from Michigan and Canada—just to watch him play."

Travis and Grandma sat in the chair for a long time, not saying anything. Grandma was smiling and looking off into the distance, watching a game he couldn't see.

At last she looked at Travis and said, "Time for bed, young man. Morning will come way too early."

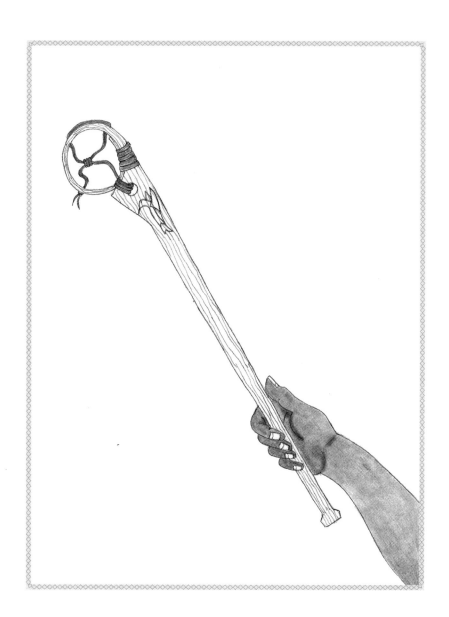

"Hello, son. What are you up to?" Grandpa stood at the foot of Travis's bed. Travis had fallen asleep reading a comic.

"Nothing, *Nimishoomis*. Just getting ready for bed." Travis took off his shirt and slipped on his pajamas. "What's that?"

His grandfather held a short wooden stick in his hand. Leather thongs formed a web in the center of its round head.

"This is the lacrosse stick my grandfather gave me when I was a boy. It's the kind of stick we played with back in the old days, before your mom was born." Grandpa lifted the stick toward the light and looked down its length. A hummingbird was carved into its shaft, just under a couple of strips of black tape.

"That doesn't look anything like mine," Travis said, looking at his stick leaning against the bedroom wall. Its metal shaft was topped with a large plastic head strung with stiff mesh.

"No, traditional sticks are different from modern sticks. Every tribe had its own style. The Iroquois who used to come here to play against us used long wooden sticks with a curved head, shaped a lot like your modern stick. The Cherokee played the game with two short hickory sticks, grabbing the ball almost like they were using tongs. These traditional forms of the game are still played today, with the traditional equipment."

"The ball was different in the old days, too," Grandpa said, reaching into his pocket and pulling out a small, worn,

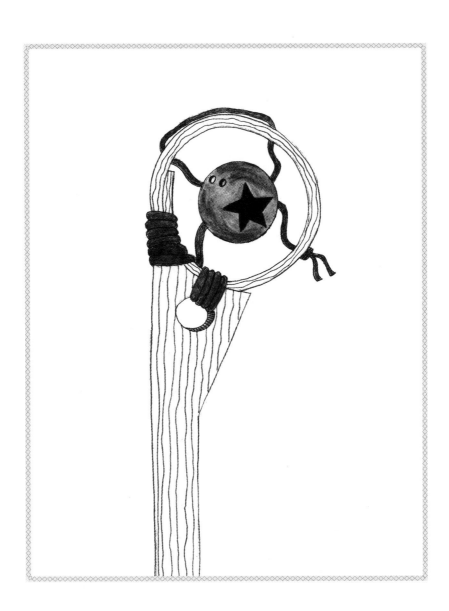

wooden ball, painted red and white. "The *bikwaawad* was made from the knob of a tree. This one here has a couple of holes in it so that it whistled as it flew through the air. My Cherokee friends played with a different sort of ball. Theirs was made of deer hair wrapped tightly in leather. They used their sticks to move the ball down the field, sometimes running along a stream or through the woods. They scored points for hitting the other team's goalpost with their stick or with the ball. They got more points if they hit the carved fish at the top of the goal. Only the most skilled players could hit the fish."

Grandpa handed the ball to Travis. "Hand me your ball. I want to see how heavy it is."

Travis tossed Grandpa the ball and sat back down on his bed.

"Indian people have been playing *baaga'adowe* since the beginning of time, but the game keeps evolving," Grandpa said, tossing Travis's hard rubber ball in the air and catching it. "Today, you play the game outside on the soccer field behind your school. Box lacrosse players play the game indoors on a converted hockey rink. The rules are slightly different between the indoor and outdoor game. But it is still the same game that the Thunderbirds gave to us when the earth was young and still forming."

Travis yawned and stretched before handing the *bikwaawad* back to his grandfather.

"I'd better let you get to sleep, *Waabooz*," Grandpa said as he stepped back into the shadows.

Next morning, Travis could see his breath in the car as he rode with Grandma to school.

"So, did *Gimishoomis* visit you again last night?" Grandma asked, as she turned the old car and accelerated. Travis nodded.

"How did he look?"

"Good, Grandma. Grandpa told me about the old-fashioned way of playing lacrosse. He told me about our connection to the game," Travis said, pausing. "But that doesn't change anything. I'm still no good at it. I'm small. I'm slow. And I can't throw the ball right."

His grandmother smiled, her dark eyes sparkling. "Be patient, Trav. Even your grandfather was clumsy and slow when he started the game. But he got better with practice. He kept improving as his grandfather taught him more about the game. Keep at it and work hard. You'll get better. You'll see."

They pulled up in front of Travis's school. Cars and buses lined up and spilled their passengers out onto the sidewalk like colorful confetti.

Travis grabbed his bag and stick and reached over to open the door.

"Hey, the next time *Gimishoomis* comes to visit, ask him to tell you about the time the animals played the Ball Game. That's a good one!" Grandma said. "See you at the game after school. Play hard!"

The first game of the lacrosse season came on a cool spring afternoon. Travis pulled on his white jersey with the royal blue letters over his shoulder pads. He walked down to the field and took his place on the sidelines as the two teams faced off. He didn't expect to play much, if at all.

Travis watched as Billy and Tommy ran the ball down the field, passing it almost effortlessly before Tommy fired it into the goal. The scene was repeated over and over for more than three quarters, with several players scoring goals. As the fourth period started, the Eagles led the visiting team, the Bulldogs, by a score of 15–6.

"Travis and Cody, grab your sticks and go in for the midfielders at the next whistle," Coach Deeley said.

Travis's hands were sweaty in his gloves. His heart felt like it was trying to claw its way out through his pads and jersey.

He and Cody ran out onto the field and took their positions. The Bulldogs had the ball and tried to pass it down the field. Cody snatched it out of the air with his stick and yelled, "Go, Travis, head for the goal!"

Travis ran, and Cody threw him the ball. Travis turned and found Tommy in front of the net. He threw the ball. Tommy fired and scored.

"Nice throw, klutz," Tommy sneered at him.

After the game, Travis walked alone to the car. He had played better, but that didn't really matter. He still hated lacrosse.

The smells of supper hung strong in the air: frying dough and chili that had cooked slowly in Grandma's big cast-iron pot. Fry bread usually made Travis warm and happy. But tonight he just poked at his food. He let the soft bread grow cold and left more than half a bowl of chili at his place when he pushed away from the table.

"Aren't you feeling well, little man?" Mom asked.

"I'm fine," Travis said as he walked toward his bedroom. "I'm just a little tired."

He sat down on his bed cross-legged and stared at his lacrosse bag. He sat silently for a long time. He heard Mom's bedroom door close. Soon after, Grandma turned off the television and settled in on the big sofa in the living room. The light shining under Travis's door went out.

"How are you, Trav?" asked Grandpa from the shadows.

"I'm okay," Travis said, as Grandpa walked over to sit on the edge of the bed. "Are you really here, Grandpa? Or am I just dreaming?"

"What do you think?"

"I don't know," Travis said, tilting his head to the side and looking at his grandfather. "I know you died a long time ago, but here you are, talking to me. I want to believe you're really here," he said wistfully.

"I'm here, if you believe that I am," said Grandpa, patting Travis on the knee. "What should we talk about tonight?"

"Tell me about the time the animals played lacrosse," Travis said, brightening.

"This is a story the old men told me when I was a boy:

"One day, a long time ago—no one knows exactly when, but before there were people—on the shores of Ball Club Lake, the animals of the earth challenged the animals of the sky to a game of *baaga'adowe*. The animals of the earth—the bears, wolves, moose, lynx, even the walleye—had seen the Thunderbirds playing the game with a ball made of lightning.

"The animals of the sky—the birds, the bats, the insects, the flying squirrels—had never been beaten in the ball game.

"A Spirit Being, neither of the earth nor of the sky, threw the ball into the air and the game began. *Migizi* the eagle grabbed the ball and flew toward the goal guarded by *Makwa* the bear. But before he could swoop in and touch his stick to the short post with a red ribbon tied to the top, *Bizhiw* the lynx reached up and knocked the ball loose. It rolled into the lake where *Ogaa* the walleye caught it and swam toward the sky animals' goal at the other end of the lake.

"As *Ogaa* threw the ball toward *Nigig* the otter, who was standing on shore, *Gekek* the hawk swooped in and snatched the ball out of the air.

"'Throw it to me. Throw it to me!' shouted *Nenookaasii* the hummingbird.

"'No, you're too small and weak to carry the ball to the goal,' replied *Gekek*.

"*Nenookaasii*'s wings drooped and he sank down, hovering just above the grass.

"*Gekek* flew like an arrow toward the goal. Just as he reached out the stick clutched in his sharp talons,

Ma'iingan the wolf grabbed the ball in his mouth and began to run in the opposite direction.

"And so the game progressed, with players from each team grabbing the ball and running toward the goal, only to lose the ball to the other team just before scoring.

"'Throw it to me! Throw it to me!' shouted an excited *Nenookaasii,* as he darted from tree to ground and back to tree again.

"Finally, the ball was lying loose on the ground while *Mooz* the moose and *Zhagaskaandawe* the flying squirrel scuffled.

"Seeing his chance, *Nenookaasii* buzzed down and scooped the ball into the head of his stick. He flew up toward the sun and then, reversing course, flitted down to the surface of the lake. As the animals of the earth dashed toward him, he darted to a nearby blueberry bush, then flew quick circles around the opposing players while making his way down the field. At last, *Nenookaasii* touched the goalpost with his stick and shouted, 'Point!'

"The hummingbird, one of the smallest members of his team, had won the game for the animals of the sky. You don't have to be the biggest or strongest or bravest player to win the game. You only need to know your strengths and play to them. Just like *Nenookaasii* did."

Travis nodded and smiled, but he couldn't keep his eyes open. He drifted off to sleep, dreaming of animals playing the Creator's Game.

Travis woke feeling rested, even though he had been up listening to his grandfather's stories most of the night. He threw his pajamas in a pile in the corner and pulled on his jeans and sweatshirt.

"Hello, sleepyhead," his mother said, as she stirred the scrambled eggs and cheese. "Hungry?"

"Yeah," Travis said as he sat down next to Grandma.

"How did your grandpa look last night?" Grandma asked as she leaned over to kiss Travis on the forehead.

Mom rolled her eyes and dumped the eggs onto an old, chipped platter.

"Stop it, Mom. You're just encouraging him," Travis's mother said.

Grandma stood up from the table and walked into the laundry room. She came back carrying an old blue duffle bag, wisps of dust dancing in the sun behind her.

"Here," she said, handing the bag to Travis. "This is your grandfather's old lacrosse gear."

Travis unzipped the bag and pulled out a pair of padded cloth gloves and a Ball Club Lacrosse jersey. An old helmet and a pair of black high-top sneakers rested in the bottom of the bag.

"That's all of your grandfather's gear," said Grandma. "Well, all except his stick. We buried him with that so he could play *baaga'adowe* for the Creator. You'd better get ready. We have to leave for school, and I have to get to work."

Travis sat distracted in class all day, thinking about the stories his grandfather had told him. He daydreamed about

29

the lacrosse gear in Grandpa's old bag, drawing pictures in the margins of his schoolbooks of people and animals playing the game.

When the last bell rang at the end of the day, Travis couldn't get out to the lacrosse field behind the school fast enough.

He opened his gym bag and pulled out his grandfather's gloves and jersey. The gloves were longer than his normal pair and rode up higher on his arms. But they made his hands feel almost electric. He pulled on the Ball Club Lacrosse jersey, which hung down to the middle of his thighs, and ran onto the field.

Tommy Fiorella threw a ball at Travis from across the field. Travis raised his stick and caught it, then spun and threw it back, a perfect throw to Tommy.

"Nice throw, Skinaway," Tommy yelled. Tommy's eyes were wide behind his mask.

Coach Deeley smiled. "Someone's been hitting the wall," he said. "Remember, guys, this game is all catching and throwing. You only get better with practice."

The rest of practice sped by, and Travis couldn't wait to tell Mom and Grandma how he had done.

At dinner, Travis was still wearing his grandfather's jersey.

"You'd better turn in early, player," Grandma said with a wink, as she took another sip of black coffee. "Big game tomorrow. I want you to score me a goal."

Travis hopped up off the couch, kissed his mom and grandma, and headed for his bedroom.

"Sleep tight, *Waabooz,*" Mom said.

Travis yanked off his pants and pulled on his pajama bottoms but left on his grandfather's jersey. He walked over to his gym bag and pulled out his grandfather's gloves. He slid them on and crawled into bed.

"Hey, *Waabooz,* I think I recognize that gear," Grandpa said as he shook Travis awake. "Big game tomorrow. Nervous?"

"No, Grandpa, I'm all right. I'm excited," Travis answered as he rubbed his eyes with the back of his glove. "Can you teach me some Ojibwe words about lacrosse?"

"Sure. You know, I didn't even speak English until I went to school, so Ojibwe is the language I think and dream in," Grandpa said. "Our words make me see pictures in my mind, so when I say '*baaga'adowe,*' I picture two ball players bumping hips in a game.

"We used to play the game at Leech Lake on the shores of *Baaga'adowaan-zaaga'igan,* or Ball Club Lake. You already know the word *bikwaawad,* which is the wooden ball we played with. That word makes me think of the knob on a tree, which we used to cut off and fashion into a ball. We called the stick *baaga'adowaan.* You can hear where that came from, can't you?"

Travis nodded sleepily.

"Now you'd better get back to sleep" said Grandpa. "Tomorrow's a big day."

The fans, shading their eyes with raised hands and folded newspapers, sat in colorful folding chairs arranged like a row of wildflowers on the edge of the lacrosse field.

Travis carefully drew his pads, helmet, and school jersey out of his bag and put them on. He then laced on Grandpa's gloves and picked his stick up out of the short grass at his feet. Coach Deeley sent the starters out to their positions and watched the faceoff. Quickly, the Eagle Ridge team was up by three goals.

"Can I go in, Coach?" Travis asked.

"Not yet, Skinaway. You'll go in at midfield."

After halftime, with his team up 17–5, Travis tried to be patient as he rocked from his right foot to his left and hefted his stick in both gloved hands. Didn't the coach know how much he had improved? Would Coach Deeley even put him in before the end of the game? Time was running out.

Finally, the coach yelled. "Okay, Skinaway, you're in!"

As he ran out onto the field, Travis heard a voice from the opposite sidelines. "Go, *Waabooz!* Get me a goal!" Grandma had a smile as bright and large as the sun.

Barry Amos threw the ball down the field to Tommy Fiorella, who darted and spun around several defenders but couldn't get a clear shot. He whirled and passed the ball to Travis. Travis stood in place for a brief moment before cutting toward the goal. His arms and hands, as if they had minds of their own, drew his stick back and fired at the net. The goalie lifted his shoulder to block the shot, but he wasn't quick enough.

"Goal!" shouted Tommy, who ran toward Travis with a

grin. "Nice shooting, cowboy!" Barry Amos trotted by and bumped fists with Travis. "Way to go, Trav!"

Grandma was out of her chair and jumping.

Travis had never felt happier in his life. It might not have been the winning goal, but it was a goal all the same. And it was Travis's first goal.

"How much ice cream do you think you can eat, young man?" Mom asked, as Travis and Grandma returned to their table with his second huge banana split of the evening. "You're going to be sick."

"Ahh, let him be, sweetie," Grandma said with a smile. "He earned this celebration by scoring his grandma a goal today."

Travis grinned as he shoveled a mouthful of ice cream and hot fudge into his mouth. He liked all kinds of ice cream sundaes, but banana splits were his absolute favorite. Grandpa used to take him to the ice cream parlor in town every Saturday. They would try to see how many banana splits they could consume in one sitting. And Grandpa would tell Travis stories from his childhood at Leech Lake: tales of ricing with his own grandfather and of trapping, fishing, and making maple syrup.

"I bet you can't wait to tell your grandpa about your goal," Grandma said, as if reading Travis's mind.

His mother rolled her eyes. "Please don't, Mom. Don't encourage him. He needs to know the difference between daydreams and real life. Real life is hard enough for us without a head full of ghosts and nonsense."

"Dreamtime is just as real as awake time, I keep telling you. You used to know that when you were a little girl. But you've forgotten," Grandma replied.

"And then I turned toward the goal. I was nervous. I could see the goalie's eyes through his mask as he stared at me and raised his stick. I fired the ball, and it shot past the goalie. I scored, Grandpa! I got a goal!"

Grandfather sat on the edge of the bed and watched his excited grandson replay the moment over and over. His face shone with pride.

"I'm proud of you, *Waabooz*. You never gave up, and you worked hard. Wait here a minute. I'll be right back."

Grandpa walked across the room into the shadows. Travis squinted, but he could no longer make out his grandfather's form in the dark room.

When he returned to the side of Travis's bed, Grandpa held his lacrosse stick with the hummingbird carved in the shaft.

"Here, *Waabooz*. I want you to have this. One day, you can give it to your grandson when you tell him about the importance of lacrosse to our people."

Travis took the stick, which seemed to vibrate in his hands. He looked up into his grandfather's dark eyes.

"*Miigwech*, Grandpa. Thank you. Even though this is a dream, I will always remember your gift."

Grandpa hugged him, then turned silently and walked back into the shadows.

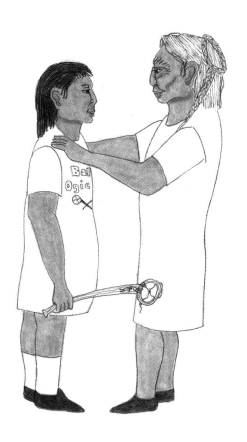

Travis slept soundly, dreaming about warm grass and wind blowing through his hair as he ran down the field behind his school. All through the night, Travis scored goal after goal with his grandfather's worn wooden stick. He heard the shouts of the crowd and his teammates as the ball found the net time after time.

"Wake up, sleepyhead. We don't want to be late again," Grandma said, poking her head into his room. She was already dressed, with her hair neatly brushed.

Travis sprang from his bed and headed for the door. "Morning, Grandma."

"What in the world is that?" Grandma asked, as she backed into the kitchen and pointed to Travis's hands. Her eyes were wide with disbelief. She couldn't speak.

Travis looked down and stopped in his tracks.

It couldn't be. Could it?

There, in his hands, was his grandfather's lacrosse stick. The stick from his dreams.

"See," Grandma said, regaining her voice. "I told you dreamtime was real. Your grandfather must have been impressed. He has given you quite a gift."

"Yes," Travis said. "He sure has."

Glossary of Ojibwe Words and Related Terms Used in the Book

Miigwech to Dr. Anton Treuer for supplying the Ojibwe pronunciations and translation assistance

Anishinaabe (uh-nish-i-nah-bay): The name for native people who live in northern Minnesota, Wisconsin, Michigan, and Canada. Also known as Ojibwe and Chippewa.

Baaga'adowaan (bah-guh-uh-doe-wahn): Lacrosse stick

Baaga'adowe (bah-guh-uh-doe-way): Lacrosse

Ball Club: A town in Minnesota on the Leech Lake Reservation. Its Ojibwe name, *Baaga'adowaaning,* means "the place where you play lacrosse."

Ball Club Lake: A lake in Ball Club, known as *Baaga'adowaan-zaaga'igan* in Ojibwe. Ojibwe people played lacrosse on both sides of the lake and held tournaments with neighboring tribes there.

Bikwaawad (bih-kwah-kwud): The knob of a tree; also, a lacrosse ball

Bizhiw (bih-zhew): Lynx

Gekek (gay-gayk): Hawk

Gimishoomis (gih-mih-show-mis): Your grandfather

Leech Lake: An Ojibwe reservation in northern Minnesota

Ma'iingan (mah-ing-un): Wolf

Makwa (muh-kwuh): Bear

Migizi (mih-gih-zee): Eagle

Miigwech (mee-gwaych): Thank you

Mooz (mooz): Moose

42

Nenookaasii (nay-noo-kah-see): Hummingbird; the nickname of Travis's grandfather, in recognition of his speed and skill at dodging defenders on the lacrosse field

Nigig (nih-gihg): Otter

Nimishoomis (nih-mih-show-mis): My grandfather

Ogaa (oh-gah): Walleye

Ogichidaa (oh-gih-chi-dah): Warrior

Ogichidaag (oh-gih-chi-dog): Warriors

Ojibwemowin (oh-jih-bway-mo-win): The Ojibwe language still spoken by some Anishinaabe people.

Ricing: To harvest wild rice, or *manoomin*, Anishinaabe people use canoes to get to wild rice beds in Minnesota lakes. Then they use a pair of knockers, or small wooden poles, to gently knock the rice from the heads of the rice plant into the bottom of the boat. After the harvest, the rice is dried on woven mats or sheets of birch bark called *apakwaan*. The rice is then parched, or roasted, often in large cast-iron kettles. After it is parched, the rice is hulled, then winnowed, or cleaned, using a birch-bark tray called a *nooshkaachinaagan*.

Spirit Being: A being that is neither human nor animal, but of the Spirit World

Thunderbirds: Ancient Spirit Beings who brought the game of lacrosse to the Anishinaabe people. According to Ojibwe stories, the older Thunderbirds invented the game to keep the young Thunderbirds busy.

Waabooz (wah-booze): Rabbit; Travis's nickname

Zhagaskaandawe (zhuh-gus-kaahn-duh-way): Flying squirrel

43

Equipment

Several versions of the game of lacrosse are played today. Native people still play traditional versions of the game, including Iroquois traditional lacrosse and the stickball game played by the Cherokee and other southeast tribes. The modern men's game is played both outdoors (field lacrosse) and indoors on modified hockey rinks (box lacrosse). Women play a version of the sport that involves less physical contact, uses different equipment, and follows different rules. Below is a description of the equipment used by modern players.

Sticks. The game of lacrosse is named for the crosse, or stick, players use to advance the ball up the field and score. In the modern outdoor men's game, players use different types of sticks, depending on the position they play.

The shaft of a goalie's stick is topped with a large head shaped like an upside-down teardrop. The plastic head is strung with mesh. Defenders and some midfielders use a stick with a longer shaft. The heads of defensive and attack sticks are smaller than the heads of goalie sticks. They can be strung with mesh or in traditional style, using string and leather. Shafts can be made of many types of materials, including wood. But most modern players look for strength and light weight in their shaft materials, choosing aluminum, titanium, or carbon fiber.

In the modern indoor game, called box lacrosse, both defensive and offensive players use the same kind of sticks. Goalie stick shafts are often longer.

Women's sticks are shorter than men's sticks, with a head that is strung traditionally, without mesh or an indented "pocket."

Safety Gear. Lacrosse helmets are worn by all players and at all levels in men's lacrosse, but only by goalies in women's lacrosse. Helmets are made of hard plastic, with a metal face mask, thick padding inside, and plenty of air holes for ventilation. Men are also required to wear chinstraps and mouth guards. Women wear eye protection and mouth guards.

Gloves. Men's and women's gloves also differ. Men's gloves, because of the amount of checking in the game, are more thickly padded than women's gloves. Only goalies are required to wear gloves in the women's game. Men's gloves are thickly padded on the back of the hand and forearm and are made of leather or canvas. Goalie gloves for both men and women are often more heavily padded around the thumb for added protection.

Pads. Men playing all positions wear pads on their arms, shoulders, and upper body. Goalies are required to wear a chest protector and throat guard in addition to a helmet and gloves. Box lacrosse goalies wear bulkier pads, like those of hockey goalies, including knee and leg guards. Men's field lacrosse goalies rarely wear leg protection. Women players, except for the goalie, don't usually wear pads. In addition to helmet and mouth guard, women goalies must wear a throat protector, padded gloves, and chest protector. Some wear arm, leg, shoulder, and chest pads.

Shoes. Men and women field lacrosse players wear cleats. Their shoes are often high tops. Men indoor players wear similar shoes, but without the cleats.

For Further Reading

Bruchac, Joseph. *Children of the Longhouse*. New York: Puffin Books, 1998.

Bruchac, Joseph. *The Warriors*. Minneapolis: Lerner Publications, 2004.

Bruchac, Joseph, and Susan L. Roth. *The Great Ball Game: A Muskogee Story*. New York: Dial Books for Young Readers, 1994.

Fink, Noah, and Melissa Gaskill. *Lacrosse: A Guide for Parents and Players*. Austin, TX: Mansion Grove House, 2006.

Hinkson, Jim. *Lacrosse Fundamentals*. Chicago: Triumph Books, 2012.

Lewis, Wendy A. *Lacrosse Warrior: The Life of Mohawk Lacrosse Champion Gaylord Powless*. Toronto: Lorimer Recordbooks, 2008.

Tucker, Janine, and Maryalice Yakutchik. *Women's Lacrosse: A Guide for Advanced Players and Coaches*. Baltimore: Johns Hopkins University Press, 2008.

Vennum, Thomas. *American Indian Lacrosse: Little Brother of War*. Baltimore: Johns Hopkins University Press, 2008.

Vennum, Thomas. *Lacrosse Legends of the First Americans*. Baltimore: Johns Hopkins University Press, 2007.

Yeager, John M. *Our Game: The Character and Culture of Lacrosse*. Port Chester, NY: Dude Publishing, 2006.

Zogry, Michael J. *Anetso, the Cherokee Ball Game: At the Center of Ceremony and Identity*. First Peoples: New Directions in Indigenous Studies. Raleigh: University of North Carolina Press, 2010.